Secret People in America

BTR Zone (Bridge to Reading) is published by Capstone Classroom,
1710 Roe Crest Drive, North Mankato, Minnesota 56003
www.capstoneclassroom.com

ISBN: 978-1-62521-066-1

Editorial Credits
Carrie Braulick Sheely, editor; Eric Manske, designer; Eric Gohl, media researcher

Photo Credits
Alamy: North Wind Picture Archives, 47, 53, 54, Paul Gooney, 57; AP Photo: Alex Brandon, 36, The News Tribune/Peter Haley, 16, Ron Edmonds, 39; Capstone Studio: Karon Dubke, 44; Corbis: Bettmann, 30, 32, Jeffrey L. Rotman, 27; Dreamstime: Aleksandar Andjic, 24; George Bush Presidential Library: 20; Getty Images: The Bridgeman Art Library, 12, Christoph Wilhelm, 22; iStockphotos: nicolecioe, 7; Landov: Dennis Brack, 26; Library of Congress: 11, 15, 31, 33, 34, 48, 49; Newscom: Everett Collection, 29, Getty Images/AFP/Paul J. Richards, 41, Getty Images/AFP/Saul Loeb, 6, ZUMA Press/Stan Godlewski, 19; Public Domain: 42; Shutterstock: BortN66, 50, Eugene Berman, 35, iofoto, 4, Joe Ravi, 8, Paul Paladin, 17; SuperStock: Jon Feingersh Photography, cover; Wikimedia: Thomas Hart, 28

Design Elements: Shutterstock

About the Cover
A man looks over his shoulder on a Washington, D.C. street.

Printed in the United States of America in North Mankato, Minnesota.
032013 007223CGF13

TABLE OF CONTENTS

CHAPTER 1

Keeping Secrets

They hide in underground tunnels and meet behind locked doors. They use fake names and work undercover.

America has always been filled with mysterious people. Many **founding fathers** were members of secret societies like the Freemasons. Even some of today's leaders are members of the secret society Skull and Bones.

Some of the first American spies worked during the American Revolutionary War (1775–1883). American **colonists** fought this war to break free of Great Britain's rule. Great Britain wanted to keep its colonies in North America. Spies worked in support of both sides. American spies had to be especially careful because they didn't know who they could trust. Several people in the colonies remained loyal to Great Britain.

founding father • a leader who helped form the United States

colonist • a person who settles in a new territory that is governed by his or her home country; the settled area is called a colony

Today the United States has official organizations that spy and do other secret work. Every day we count on spies and other members of the Central Intelligence Agency (CIA) to keep our country safe. The National Security Agency (NSA) breaks enemy **codes**. It also makes codes to keep secret U.S. information safe. But few people understand just how these organizations conduct their work. Get ready to learn the truth about the secret people in America.

lobby of the CIA headquarters building in Langley, Virginia

code • a system of letters, symbols, and numbers used to send secret messages

Secret People Just Below Our Feet

Some people claim there is a secret world deep beneath New York City. They estimate more than 5,000 people live underground in the city's empty subway tunnels. The citizens who live in these tunnels are called mole people. It's possible some mole people have lived underground for more than 10 years. People claim they have formed an organized society with communities of leaders, teachers, and nurses.

The George Washington Masonic Memorial in Virginia is a meeting place for members of a secret society called the Freemasons. It also honors Freemason and founding father George Washington.

CHAPTER 2

Secret Societies

Secret societies keep their actions and members' identities hidden from others. Meeting places are top secret, and membership is **exclusive**. Some groups make each member take an oath, or a formal promise to do something. Others perform fancy **rituals** at each meeting.

Because the groups are so mysterious, they raise many questions. Who can join them? Why do they exist? And why do they insist on being so secretive?

exclusive • limiting; exclusive groups allow only certain people to become members

ritual • an action that is always performed in the same way

Sons of Liberty

In 1765 America was part of Great Britain. When Britain needed more money, the king forced the American colonists to pay **taxes**. The colonists did not want to pay the new taxes.

Storekeepers and artists from Boston hoped to put an end to the taxes. They were known as the Loyal Nine. Word of the group spread, and more people wanted to join. The group then became known as the Sons of Liberty.

Being part of the Sons of Liberty was dangerous. The group met in secret so members wouldn't get caught. Some members committed **treason**. They damaged British cargo ships and spoke out against the government. The punishment for treason was death.

tax • money collected from a country's citizens to help pay for running the government

treason • the act of betraying one's country

a Sons of Liberty meeting in New York, December 17, 1773

Fact

In 1765 American colonists met under a huge elm tree in Boston, Massachusetts. They were displaying their anger about a British tax called the Stamp Act. The tree later became known as the Liberty Tree. Sons of Liberty members regularly met under it.

The Sons of Liberty wanted to protest the Tea Act passed in 1773. The act said only the British East India Company could sell tea to the colonists. By law, colonists had to pay a tax on the tea. At the time, tea was the drink of choice in the colonies. Most colonists drank at least two cups of tea every day. The Tea Act made the colonists furious.

the Boston Tea Party

In December 1773 the Sons of Liberty boarded three ships that carried tea from Britain. **Disguised** as American Indians, they dumped more than 300 chests of tea into the Boston Harbor. They knew no one would believe they were Indians. Instead, they hoped their costumes would keep them from being recognized. This event became known as the Boston Tea Party.

The Sons of Liberty convinced many colonists to fight against British laws. Disagreements between colonists and British rulers eventually led to the Revolutionary War.

Fact

People who supported the colonists' fight for freedom before and during the Revolutionary War were called patriots. Famous patriots Paul Revere and Samuel Adams were members of the Sons of Liberty.

disguise • to hide one's real identity, often by using clothes and makeup

The Freemasons

After the American colonists won the Revolutionary War, there were important choices to make. What would the new government be like? Who would lead the country? Many leaders stepped forward with answers. Some of these leaders, such as Benjamin Franklin and George Washington, belonged to a secret group called the Freemasons.

The Freemasons is a very old society. Most people agree that a group of **stonemasons** started the organization in London in 1717. Others think that the group is much older.

People from England continued the Freemason group when they came to the American colonies. These Freemasons helped to establish the United States. Several Freemasons signed the Declaration of Independence.

stonemason • someone who builds or works with stone

constitution • the written system of laws in a country that state the rights of people and the powers of government

Members of the Freemasons sometimes wear special clothing for important events.

Approved on July 4, 1776, it stated that the 13 colonies were free of Great Britain. Thirteen signers of the U.S. **Constitution** were also Freemasons.

officers of the Prince Hall
Freemason group, 2003

Despite their important role in American history, Freemasons are still considered very mysterious. About 5 million Freemason members exist throughout the world. Their meetings are open only to members. They share secret passwords and handshakes.

Freemasons participate in rituals called Masonic degrees. These ceremonies are held in special lodges (meeting places) and include music, costumes, and props.

The mysteries surrounding the Freemasons have some people very concerned. These people worry that the Freemasons have too much power in government. A few people even believe they are trying to take over the world.

Freemasons consider themselves private but not secret. They do not hide the fact that they are members. Yet few people know what actually happens behind the closed doors of their lodges.

Freemason Symbols

Look closely at the back of a dollar bill. You'll see a pyramid and an eye. These designs are similar to Freemason symbols. That's because some of the leaders responsible for choosing national symbols were Freemasons. They picked familiar images. The pyramid and the eye symbolize that the United States is still unfinished.

Skull and Bones Society

The Skull and Bones society is one of the oldest and most secretive groups in America. Its members are called Bonesmen. They meet in a windowless building nicknamed the Tomb. Some people claim that the Tomb is decorated with human skulls.

In 1832 students at Yale University in New Haven, Connecticut, started the Skull and Bones Society. Each year some of the most successful students at Yale are invited to join. Their members have become very successful judges, **politicians**, and businesspeople. Maybe that's because members promise to help one another succeed. Bonesmen help other Skull and Bones members get jobs and leadership positions.

Members voted in 1991 to allow women to become Bonesmen. Before that time, only men could be members. Other than that, little has changed since the group formed. Each year 15 people are invited to join during a nighttime ceremony. Members are given special nicknames.

politician • a person who is part of government or runs for a government position

Fact

Yale University is home to several other secret organizations in addition to the Skull and Bones.

the Tomb

George H. W. Bush (standing left of clock) with other Skull and Bones members

Some people worry about how much power the Bonesmen have. That's because many Bonesmen have held important government positions. Three former U.S. presidents were Bonesmen. They are William Taft, George H. W. Bush, and George W. Bush. Secretary of State John Kerry is also a member.

Geronimo's Skull

In 2009 the family of the well-known Apache Indian warrior Geronimo filed a lawsuit against the Skull and Bones society. The family members said Bonesmen stole Geronimo's skull in 1918. They then took the skull to the Tomb, where it is kept in a glass box. According to the story, one of the robbers was Prescott Bush, the father of former president George H. W. Bush.

In 2005 a historian found a letter from one Bonesman to another. The letter mentions a skull taken from Fort Sill, where Geronimo died as a prisoner. Despite this **evidence**, the case was dismissed (taken out of the court system) in 2010.

evidence • information, items, and facts that help prove something to be true or false

CHAPTER 3

Sneaky Spies

Imagine going on dangerous missions like James Bond and other spy movie characters. Movie makers pack scenes with action for our entertainment. But real-life spies around the world risk their lives every day. They will do almost anything to get the job done right. Many spies protect their countries by secretly watching the actions of enemy countries. They gather secret information they hope will be valuable to their countries' interests (concerns). Employees of the CIA are constantly at work in support of the United States.

But not all spies are loyal to their countries. **Double agents** cross the line between helping their country and betraying it. They trade information to other countries. If caught, the punishment can be death. A few CIA spies have become known for their betrayal.

double agent • a spy who works for one country's government but is really loyal to another

CIA Spies

The CIA calls its spies operations officers. Their jobs are some of the agency's most secretive and dangerous positions. These undercover (secret) spies travel the world gathering secret information.

The CIA was created in 1947 to collect **intelligence** in foreign countries. During the 1960s the CIA gathered information that kept dangerous weapons out of foreign countries. CIA spies also collected information that helped U.S. soldiers fighting in the Vietnam War (1959–1975). Today the CIA gathers information on everything from suspected **terrorists** to **mobsters** and illegal drug dealers.

a lie detector test being performed

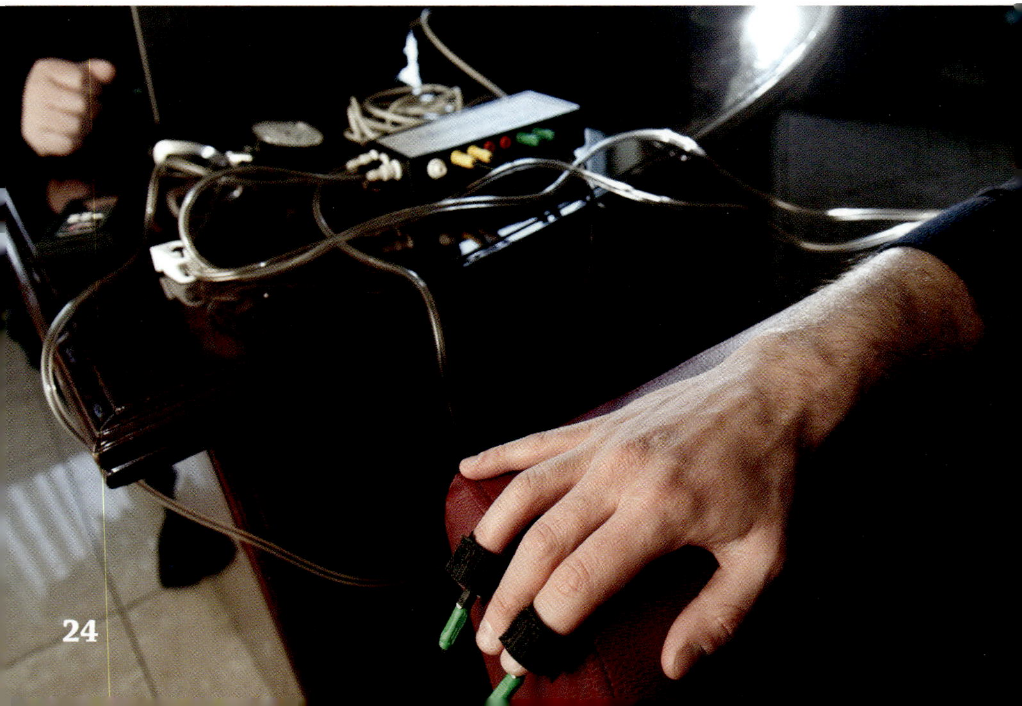

More than 10,000 people apply to work for the CIA each month. Besides undercover spies, the CIA has many positions. They range from scientists who create high-tech gear to analysts who study information. Not everyone can work for the CIA. To be considered for a job, candidates must be U.S. citizens. Most CIA employees have graduated from college. Job candidates have to pass a lie detector test and medical tests. The lengthy application process can take up to a year.

Fact

The president receives an update from the CIA each day called the President's Daily Brief.

intelligence • secret information about an enemy's plans or actions

terrorist • someone who uses violence and threats to frighten people and to achieve a political or religious goal

mobster • a member of a large criminal organization

a spy camera mounted in a shoe

CIA spies have many ways to collect information. Spies check foreign newspapers, TV reports, and radio broadcasts. Some spies use **satellites** to watch foreign leaders.

Undercover spies must create false identities. They have fake names, birthdays, and life histories. They may use makeup and clothing to disguise themselves.

Not all CIA workers collect top-secret information, though. Some spies are responsible for protecting government secrets. These people work with the Federal Bureau of Investigation (FBI) to keep U.S. military and other secrets out of enemy hands. Protecting top-secret information is called **counterintelligence**. Sometimes enemies are even given false information. The CIA hopes the phony information will confuse enemies.

Spies also have many high-tech tools to help them collect information. Photos are captured using cameras hidden in jewelry, buttons, or shoes. Tiny listening devices called bugs can be hidden just about anywhere. Bugs transmit (send) people's conversations to recording devices.

a bug hidden in a tie

satellite • a spacecraft used to send signals and information from one place to another

counterintelligence • actions designed to keep secrets safe from enemies

Double agents and traitors threaten national security. Some of these people are especially known for the damage they have caused to the United States.

Benedict Arnold

Benedict Arnold in his officer uniform

Benedict Arnold was an officer (leader) in the American army during the Revolutionary War. Some soldiers thought highly of him, but others didn't. Arnold was passed over for a more important position he thought he deserved. Arnold also struggled to pay his bills. He decided to betray his country. Arnold offered to give the British information in return for payment. Some of this information helped the British capture an American fort. The Americans found out about Arnold's betrayal. But he fled to British troops before he could be punished.

Alger Hiss

Alger Hiss just after his arrest

During World War II (1939–1945), the Soviet Union, Great Britain, and the United States were **allies**. But some Americans feared the Soviets were spying on the U.S. government. The traitor Alger Hiss fueled those fears.

Hiss worked for the U.S. State Department, which handles relations with foreign countries. In 1933 he secretly began spying for the Soviet Union. Hiss gave the Soviets details about U.S. efforts to stop Soviet spies. He also gave them information about private talks held between the United States and other countries.

In the late 1940s, Hiss was **accused** of being a spy. Hiss denied it, but later evidence pointed to his guilt. He was found guilty of lying in court about his involvement with a spy ring (group). Until his death, he continued to claim he was not a spy.

ally • a person or country that gives support to another

accuse • to say that someone has done something wrong

Klaus Fuchs

Klaus Fuchs after his prison release in 1959

The Manhattan Project was a secret U.S. military project. Its purpose was to produce the world's first **atomic bomb**. By 1942 the need for the bomb seemed clear. There were rumors that Germany was building an atomic bomb. Germany was an enemy in World War II, which was currently raging around the world. The United States was determined to build the bomb first.

The U.S. government didn't want other countries to know how to build atomic bombs. They tried to keep the information secret. But in 1950, scientist Klaus Fuchs was arrested for sharing atomic bomb secrets with the Soviet Union.

Fuchs thought the Soviet Union needed atomic weapons to defend itself. In 1945 he gave the Soviets detailed plans for making an atomic bomb. Later he sent secrets about the even deadlier hydrogen bomb.

Julius and Ethel Rosenberg

In 1951 husband and wife Julius and Ethel Rosenberg were also arrested for sharing atomic bomb-making secrets. Ethel's brother got a job where the bomb was being built. He gave Julius information. Julius then passed the information to the Soviets. The couple was sentenced to death, but people still disagree about whether or not they were guilty.

Julius and Ethel Rosenberg

atomic bomb • a powerful explosive that destroys large areas; atomic bombs leave behind harmful elements called radiation

War Spies

Some of America's most well-known spies worked during times of war. A few of these spies directly affected the outcome of battles.

Nathan Hale disguised himself as a schoolteacher while he spied.

Nathan Hale is one of the most famous spies from the Revolutionary War. Hale spied on British army camps. He drew maps of enemy camp locations. But instead of memorizing the information, he kept notes. The British found the notes when they caught Hale. Hale was killed for being a spy.

Many famous American spies conducted their dangerous duties during the American Civil War (1861–1865). This war was fought between the **Confederacy** and the **Union**. The Confederacy was made up of 11 southern states that broke away from the rest of the country in 1861. The Union was made up of northern states that wanted to keep the country together.

Allan Pinkerton

The northern and the southern states had been fighting for years over slavery and how much control individual states should have. Southern states wanted to keep slavery, while northerners wanted to do away with it. Southern states also wanted more control in government. Both sides used spies to gather information about the enemy.

Allan Pinkerton was a key figure in Union **espionage**. He set up a network of spies for Major General McClellan. Pinkerton's agents worked deeply undercover. Pinkerton even went on undercover missions himself. He worked among the Confederates and sent information back to McClellan. Meanwhile, another Union spy, Lafayette Baker, and his agents sent information to another Union general. Pinkerton and Baker worked so secretly they even kept information from each other!

Confederacy · the 11 southern states that left the Union and fought against the northern states in the Civil War

Union · the northern states that fought against the southern states in the Civil War

espionage · spying

One of the most famous Confederate spies was Belle Boyd. She persuaded Union soldiers to reveal military secrets. She once hid in a closet to overhear a Union general giving important information to his staff. She risked her own life, and that of her slave, to deliver information to the Confederates.

Belle Boyd

The United States built the U-2 spy plane in the mid-1950s.

Cold War Spying

During the Cold War (1945-1991), no weapons were actually fired. But the threats to do so were numerous. Also numerous were the number of spies used to gather information. The Cold War involved the United States and the Soviet Union. Neither side trusted the other, and each was desperate to find out what the enemy was doing. American spies gathered secrets about soviet technology. They also spied on the Soviet Union using high-flying spy planes.

Secret Service agents closely guard Barack Obama and first lady Michelle Obama in January 2009.

CHAPTER 4

Government and Military Groups

Official spies aren't the only ones who aren't open about their activities. Several official U.S. groups and agencies keep details about what they do hidden. Sometimes these secrets are kept to help protect the country. But the hidden details keep American citizens guessing about what is really going on.

Secret Service

Look carefully the next time the president speaks at an event. You might see people wearing dark suits and earpieces. They don't take their eyes off the crowd. They are members of the Secret Service.

The Secret Service has two jobs—investigation and protection. Some agents investigate crimes that involve money and computers. Other agents protect the president. They also guard presidential families, former presidents, visiting foreign leaders, and presidential candidates. People the Secret Service protects are called "protectees."

Like police officers, Secret Service agents carry guns and handcuffs. They wear radios and bulletproof vests.

When the president travels, the Secret Service works with area police forces to help ensure security. A great deal of planning goes into large events where the president appears.

True to its name, most of the agency's work remains secret. By revealing few details, the Secret Service can provide better protection to protectees.

Some Secret Service agents dress as members of the public instead of in uniforms. This practice keeps people from recognizing them. If suspects know where Secret Service members are, they can better plan an attack.

A job in Secret Service isn't just secretive—it's dangerous. In 1981 agent Tim McCarthy was wounded while protecting President Ronald Reagan from a gunman. Agent Leslie Coffelt was killed in 1950 when two people tried to shoot President Harry Truman. Coffelt is the only agent to be killed while preventing an attack.

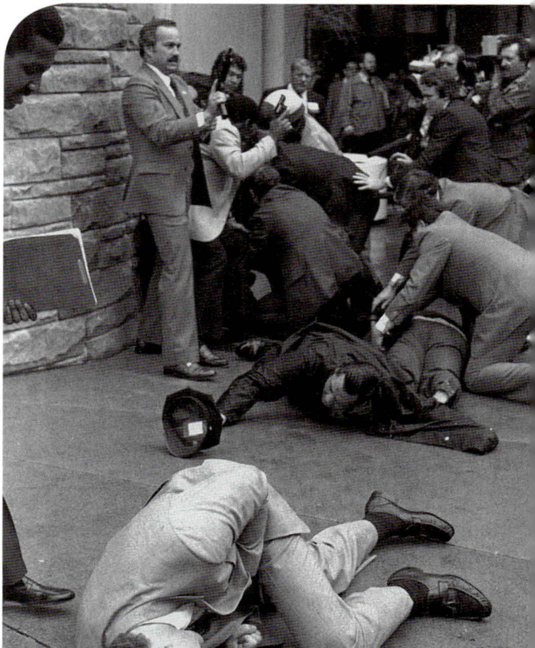

Tim McCarthy lies wounded after trying to protect President Ronald Reagan in 1981.

Fact

Agents use code names for the people they protect. President Obama's code name is "Renegade." George W. Bush's code name was "Trailblazer."

NSA

The National Security Agency (NSA) is a secretive group with a complicated mission. For years no one knew much about the NSA. People claimed the group didn't exist. They joked that NSA stood for "No Such Agency." But the NSA does exist, and its job is top secret.

In 1952 President Harry Truman created the NSA to keep track of foreign enemies. NSA workers cracked codes used during the Korean War (1950–1953) and during the Vietnam War (1959–1975).

Today workers collect information on suspected terrorists using high-tech computer systems. NSA workers listen to private conversations and gather foreign information that is usually written in code. NSA workers crack these secret codes so government leaders can use the information.

All the secrecy makes some people nervous—and with good reason. Some reports have claimed the NSA is keeping close watch on average American citizens. This includes recording millions of phone calls and collecting e-mails. But no one knows just how much information the agency is collecting or how much it already has collected.

the NSA Threat Operations Center, Fort Meade, Maryland

In 2011 the NSA began building a huge building to store data in Utah. This news worried people even more that the agency is storing personal information of American citizens. But NSA leaders have said that the agency has no interest in watching average Americans.

Navy SEALs on a training mission

Special Operations Forces

Members of the military's special operations forces (SOF) have some of the most dangerous jobs in the world. Different military branches have their own SOF groups. Some of the most well-known groups are the Navy SEALs, the Army Rangers, and the Army Special Forces, or Green Berets. All SOF groups perform secret missions, but some groups are more secretive than others. Especially secretive groups include the Army's Delta Force and the Navy's SEAL team 6.

Each SOF group has several primary (key) missions. Sometimes operatives (members) work alone, but more often they work in small teams. SOF operatives perform rescue missions and dispose of bombs before they explode. They plan surprise attacks on enemies and spy.

Sometimes operatives secretly find out information about enemies by disguising themselves. These spies dress, act, and speak as much like the local people as possible. The information they collect might help them during an investigation or in battle.

Many specific actions of SOF missions are kept secret when they are over. The public often receives few details of the missions. American citizens are then left wondering what really happened.

Fact

Special operations forces make up less than two percent of the U.S. military forces.

Since the early 1950s, some Americans have believed that the Men in Black visit those who report UFOs. They are said to scare the witnesses into silence.

CHAPTER 5

Other Secret People

Secret people don't have to be part of an official organization or group. Sometimes people never intended to be part of a secret world. These people may have ended up conducting secret activities because of their belief systems and what is happening in society. And according to some people, there might even be secretive beings around that aren't even human!

Men in Black

Late at night a strange light appears in the sky. A man calls the police to report an Unidentified Flying Object (UFO). Days later, three men wearing sunglasses and dark suits arrive at the man's door. They warn him not to talk about the UFO. This sounds like a Hollywood movie. But some people believe stories like this are very real.

Albert Bender was the first person to talk about the Men in Black (MIB). Bender ran a research group in Connecticut called the Flying Saucer Bureau. In 1953 he suddenly ended the group and his research. Bender later said that men in dark suits had visited him. They claimed to be government workers and said he must stop investigating UFOs.

Bender said the men told him the truth about UFOs. But he never told anyone what he learned. In the 1960s many people reported similar visits.

Some people say MIB agents have gray skin and wires coming out of their legs. Other people think MIB agents are really aliens. If the Men in Black do exist, no one knows who or what they really are.

The Road to Freedom

For those running the Underground Railroad, secrecy was key. Their lives depended on it. The Underground Railroad operated in the United States from about 1810 to 1840. It was a series of homes and shelters in the southern United States. People who disagreed with slavery created the route. They hid runaway slaves in their cellars, attics, and barns. They also gave runaways food and clothing.

With the help of the Underground Railroad, more than 100,000 people escaped slavery. They fled to the northern United States and to Canada, where slavery was illegal.

If caught trying to escape, slaves faced severe punishments.

The Underground Railroad had to operate in complete secrecy. Hiding slaves was a crime. Runaways who were caught were often beaten, tortured, or even killed. Many people risked their lives to make the Underground Railroad successful. Two of these people were Levi Coffin and Harriet Tubman.

Levi Coffin was known as the president of the Underground Railroad. His home was called Grand Central Station. Runaways were welcome there day or night. Coffin and his wife hid more than 2,000 slaves.

Levi Coffin

From 1850 to 1861, former slave Harriet Tubman made 19 dangerous trips to help slaves escape. The trips were not easy. She and the slaves traveled only at night. She gave children a special medicine to make them sleep so they wouldn't make any noise. In all, Tubman helped rescue about 300 slaves.

Harriet Tubman

CHAPTER 6

Mysteries in History

American history is filled with mystery. Some people's mysterious ways can be easily found in history books. Others are surrounded by secrecy. Sometimes facts are revealed, but we aren't told the whole truth.

Over the years, researchers have revealed many secrets and secret people of the past. We now know the secret routes of the Underground Railroad. We also know about people who secretly helped the slaves through the Railroad. But at the time, the slaves' mysterious disappearances confused and angered slave owners.

Despite researchers' hard work, many questions about American history remain unanswered. In these cases, it's up to you to review the facts. Then you can decide what to believe.

Roanoke Colony

One of America's well-known mysteries involves the disappearance of an English colony. In 1587 a group of people from England boarded a ship. The men, women, and children planned to start a town on Roanoke Island in North Carolina. But soon after landing, the colonists ran out of supplies.

Captain John White returned to England for more supplies. But England was at war with Spain, and ships were being used only for battles. White was unable to return to Roanoke for two years.

When he did return, White was shocked by what he found. The growing colony had disappeared. A single clue was left behind. The word "croatoan" was carved on a tree.

In 1607 more English colonists came to Virginia and settled the colony of Jamestown. The governor of Jamestown, John Smith, spoke to the local Indian chief, Powhatan, about the Roanoke colonists. Powhatan said that during a war his men attacked and killed a group of Europeans who had settled in the area. As proof he showed Smith a musket barrel, which had belonged to the Roanoke colonists.

Still Searching

The people of Jamestown continued to search for the lost colonists. They sent out two groups in 1608. Neither of the groups found evidence of the missing colonists.

John White was the first of many people to try to find out what happened to the Roanoke colonists.

What happened to the colonists? One idea is that they left to settle elsewhere. Others believe Croatoan Indians killed the colonists. But historians think it's more likely that the Indians offered to help the colonists. The Indians had enough food to keep the colonists alive. There is evidence to support this claim. Years later, Indians with gray eyes were said to have been seen in the area. Some spoke English and had English names. It's possible they were related to the Roanoke colonists.

Although most experts think the colonists went with the Indians, they want to be sure. Some researchers hope **DNA** will get them closer to cracking this case. They are testing the DNA of people they think might be related to the lost colonists. DNA testing can show what type of Native American ancestry people have in their backgrounds. DNA can also be used to help find common ancestors.

DNA · material in cells that gives people their individual characteristics, such as eye and hair color

Uncover More Secrets

This book has listed a few of the secret people in America from both past and present times. But there are countless others. The Bilderberg Club is thought to have a huge influence on business. Other groups might be so secret that we don't even know they exist.

Now it's your turn to search for America's mysterious people. Who knows what secrets you might uncover!

Would You Have What it Takes?

Do you think you might like to work with the CIA some day? This chart can help you explore what the CIA looks for in its employees. Match the color coding in each text block to the career groups at the bottom.

I like taking tough classes at school and push myself hard in sports and other activities.

Most CIA workers like to challenge themselves.

I enjoy learning about other cultures.

Understanding other cultures helps CIA officers work with people from different countries. It also helps analysts choose the best course of action.

I think telling stories and acting in plays is a lot of fun.

The abilities to play different roles and win the trust of others are key skills for CIA operations officers.

I enjoy exercising and staying fit.

CIA officers in the field need to have good physical fitness to deal with potentially dangerous situations.

I like writing reports.

No matter their position, CIA workers must be able to explain situations clearly in reports. This skill is especially important for analysts.